This journal Belongs To

From

ONLY REAL

LEGENDS

WERE BORN IN

A·P·R·I·L

1939

Happy birthday

I'm grateful that you are a part of my life. All the best on your birthday !

In good times and bad, I'll always be by your side. Happy birthday!

Happy, happy birthday ! You deserve all the cakes, love, hugs and happiness !

Drawing on my fine command of language, I said nothing

Real friends help you succeed while fake friends try to destroy your future

Fate only takes you so far. The rest is up to you

A stitch in time would have confused Einstein

He was a true friend, he stabbed me in the front

Plan like you will live forever, live like you will die tomorrow

True friendship is like a rose. We can't realize it's beauty until it fades

Success has many fathers, but failure is an orphan

It is twice as hard to crush a half-truth as a whole lie

Perhaps one day this too will be pleasant to remember

To err is human, to blame the next guy even more so

Count your life by smiles, not tears. Count your age by friends, not years

Television is chewing gum for the eyes

If you can't find the key to success, pick the lock

The tongue weighs practically nothing. But so few people can hold it

Everyone is entitled to be stupid, but some abuse the privilege

A best friend is like a four leaf clover - Hard to find, and lucky to have

The early bird gets the worm, but the second mouse gets the cheese

A gentleman is a man who can play the accordion but doesn't

Feelings are like the sunrise...different colors...different shades...each and every time

Formal education will earn you a living, self-education make you a fortune

Confidence in nonsense is a requirement for the creative process

War doesn't determine who is right, only who is left

In a world full of copycats- be an original

Life is too short to settle for anything less than a 110 effort

Everyone wants to be accepted by a world that is unacceptable

A friend is one who believes in you when you have ceased to believe in yourself

Ask not how far must I walk, instead say I will walk as far is as needed

The future belongs to those who dare

A wise man can see more from the bottom of a well than a fool can from a mountain top

Great minds think independently, not alike

Life is too short to be sensible

Where you find true friendship. You find true love

After all is said and done, a lot more will have been said than done

Don't cry because it's over smile because it happened

Don't deny hope it's chance to work magic

Education is not received. It is achieved

Character is what you are when no one is looking

Sometimes it Takes a Stranger to Understand you

He who loses faith, loses all

A closed mouth gathers no foot

An act against my will is not my act

Courage atrophies from lack of use

Everything you do or say is public relations

Life is a comedy for those who think and a tragedy for those who feel

Try and fail, but don't fail to try

We were all born with wings. In times of doubt spread them

Artificial Intelligence is no match for natural stupidity

The hardest part of any journey is taking that first step

Women remember the first kiss, men remember the last

You only live once, but if you live right, once is enough

Anarchy - it's not the law, it's just a good idea

The greatest oak was once a little nut who held its ground ....

Every oak tree started out as a couple of nuts who decided to stand their ground

The greatest oak was once a little nut who held its ground ....

Every success is built on the ability to do better than good enough

Between the wish and the thing life lies waiting

Those who stare at the past have their backs turned to the future

The more you run over a dead cat, the flatter it gets

Listen to life, it is the wisest teacher of all

Tact is the art of making a point without making an enemy

Politicians talking about honesty is like prostitutes talking about virginity

Pain is inevitable; suffering is optional

It is the darkest hour before dawn

Love is friendship caught on fire

Everyone hates change because change brings the unknown

I have not lost my mind - it's backed up on disk somewhere

All general statements are false

Failure to prepare is preparing to fail

It's difficult to lose someone than to get someone

Use disappointments as material for patience

Barnum was wrong - it's more like every 30 seconds

Beware of impostors taking sweet words

If a man yields himself to God, He will change

If all the world's a stage, then where is the audience sitting

In every fat book there is a thin book trying to get out

It takes a lot of balls to golf the way I do

Some days you're the dog, and some days you're the hydrant

Blessed are the cracked For they shall let in the light

No good plan survives contact with the enemy

Why learn at all if one day we will die and forget everything

My Karma ran over your dogma

World is full of plagiarizer

What's real in politics is what the voters decide is real

You are worth more than your darkness

Take only pictures, steal only time, leave only footprints

All power corrupts, but we need the electricity

Birds of feather flocks together

Give, and forget Receive, and remember

A library is an arsenal of liberty

Fools rush in where fools have been before

That which we obtain too easily, we esteem too lightly

Failure isn't falling. It's refusing to get back up

He who ceases to learn cannot adequately teach

Never deprive someone of hope -- it may be all they have

Practice Random Acts of Kindness and Senseless Beauty

Show a leg or shake a leg

Life was made to be enjoyed as well as endured

The only real failure in life is the failure to try

What I said never changed anyone. What they understood did

I believe in livin' a life less ordinary... Yet extraordinary

A similie: Like a duck on a June bug

Commitment in the face of conflict produces character

Sometimes the biggest risk you can take is not taking a risk

The door to opportunity is always labeled 'push'

Made in the USA
Monee, IL
27 March 2022